AMISH TRUE LOVE

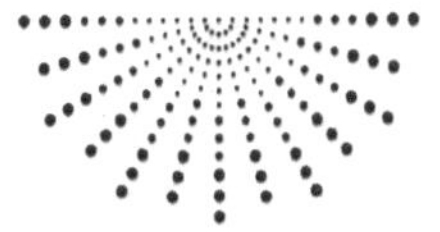

SARAH MILLER

CHAPTER ONE

There is a time for everything,
and a season for every activity under the heavens:
Ecclesiastes 3:1

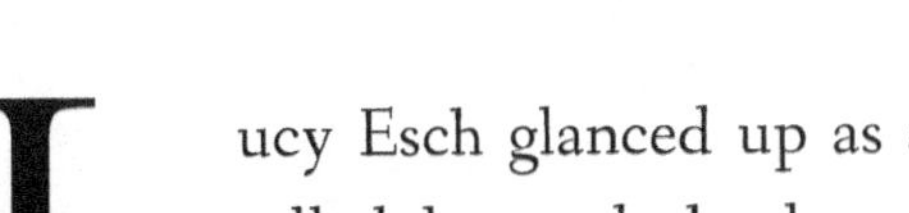

Lucy Esch glanced up as a big gray cloud rolled by, and she knew that soon, the weather would change. "Should we fetch Jacob and Joseph in?" she asked her *mamm*. "There's a storm coming."

Lucinda Esch looked up from her weeding. She was shorter than her daughter, with most of her hair now gray, but she still had a sense of fun in her life, and she chuckled at her daughter's silliness. "Those lambs have big warm coats, they will be fine. It is you, my *dochder,* with your light dress that will catch your death if you stay out too long worrying about your pets."

"Pets," Lucy said, her serious brown eyes lighting up with the hope that her dreams were coming true. "Maybe I could keep these two. They are so tame, and they would make such good pets. You could talk to *Daed* for me?"

Lucinda dropped her eyes. "You know why we keep them, it is the way. How many times have I told you not to give them names and not to get too attached?"

"*Jah,* but *Mamm,* I so want a pet, maybe a dog or a cat, just something to call my own."

Lucinda chuckled again. "Soon, you will be married and have a *haus* of your own. Then you can have as many pets as you want."

Lucy dropped the handful of herbs she had been

picking and stared at her *mamm*. What was she saying? As she watched, color spread over her *mamm's* cheeks, and she looked down guiltily. "What have you done?" Lucy asked her voice much harsher than she intended.

Lucinda continued to stare at the garden, picking out a weed here and nipping off a shoot there, but as the silence continued, she eventually looked up. Lucy's eyes bored into hers, and she knew that her slip would come back to haunt her. How could she be so stupid? "Your *daed* and I have been talking. You are old enough to marry. You have been for a while now. Recently we were discussing this with Larry Schrock. He has a son Jonas, a nice boy and we have decided that the two of you would make a *gut* match. Jonas will pick you up after dinner and you two will start courting." Lucinda felt the words stream out of her, and she could not stop them, even though each one seemed to hit Lucy with the force of a stone. Eventually, she stopped talking, and the two just stared at each other.

Lucy wore an expression of hurt and disbelief, and Lucinda wanted to comfort her daughter, to ease away the pain, but what could she say? "The marriage will be *gut* for you, and then you can have a pet." As soon as the words left her mouth, Lucinda regretted them. They were meant as a comfort but came out as callous and uncaring.

"You don't understand," Lucy slung at her *mamm*. "Marriage should be about love." With that, she dropped her basket of herbs and turned and ran.

"Lucy, Lucy come back; we can talk about this," Lucinda shouted as her daughter ran out of the garden and across the fields towards the coming storm clouds.

Lucinda hovered between running to the house or to the barn. Maybe she should harness the buggy horse and go looking for Lucy? She let her eyes follow her daughter. Already Lucy had crossed the field and was heading into the woods. No, she could not follow. Lucy needed her space, but she was a sensible girl. Though she was angry now, soon, she would turn around and come home.

A peel of thunder heralded the coming storm, and Lucinda picked up Lucy's basket of herbs and their tools and headed back to the house. If this storm kept up, the men would be back soon. They would want a warm house and a hot meal. If anything would tempt Lucy back, it would be the smell of meatloaf and fresh bread. Feeling a little better, Lucinda headed in out of the wind.

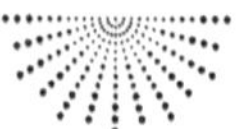

CHAPTER TWO

Even youths grow tired and weary,
and young men stumble and fall,
but those who hope in the LORD will renew their
strength.
They will soar on wings like eagles;
they will run and not grow weary,
they will walk and not be faint.
Isaiah 40:30-31

Lucy ran across the field, feeling the wind push through her thin cotton dress and apron. How could they do this? Anger fueled her as she fled away from her home, and the hurt her parents had caused. Every year they let her raise two lambs, and then they would slaughter them for meat. Every year she prayed that they would let her keep one, but they never did and every year, she got so attached that when the lambs were killed, she cried for weeks. Her daed always laughed and teased her, but he never gave in. The only thing that kept her going was knowing that one day she would look up and see the man she was to marry. Their eyes would meet and they would know. It would be powerful and instant and romantic, and she knew it would happen. She would find true love. It was the reason that she rarely courted. None of the men made her feel good, none of them caused her to have butterflies in her stomach like she read about in the books she got second hand from the store. But it would happen one day, her soul mate was out there and if she ended up married to some boy then how could it ever happen?

A branch whipped her face and caught her prayer

covering as she ran past. It ripped it from her head, and she turned to see it hanging there. The sight of it, like a wounded bird trapped in the spindly branches, made her sad. She yanked it down and pulled the bits of stick free before pulling it back onto her head. Just as she did, a raindrop hit her hand. The storm was here. Lucy wondered what to do? She would not go on this date, but if she stayed out here in the storm, then soon she would be soaked. As she walked through the trees, an idea came to her, and she ran towards the stream.

There was a hiding place, somewhere she went when she wanted to be alone. Somewhere that was dry and would keep her safe. She could hide there for a few hours and then sneak back into the house after dark. Hopefully, by tomorrow, this would have all blown over, and Jonas would realize that she would not court him.

The rain was falling heavily now, and thick black clouds covered the sky. It made it dark beneath the trees as she hurried along to find the creek. Many times, she had walked in these woods, but everything looked so different, she wondered if she was lost. Rain streamed through the trees and soaked her to the skin. Her prayer *kapp* was soaked and plastered to her head as her dress was plastered to her body. For a second, she wondered if she should go home. She could try and retrace her steps but then she heard the sound of running water. She must be close. Quickly she ran towards the sound and recognized a fallen log. All she had to do was follow the creek bed for a short distance, and she would come upon the culvert.

Rain ran off her prayer covering and into her eyes. She wiped her face with a wet sleeve as she made her way across the treacherous ground. Not much further, and at least she would be dry and out of the rain.

There up ahead, the road crossed the stream, and beneath it was a storm drain, with two concrete stanchions. She could crouch on one of them and keep out of the rain, at least for a little while. The rain poured down, making the water higher than usual. It raced beneath the bridge. Lucy slipped down the slope and grabbed onto a root to stop herself from falling into the water. It flowed past fast and angry as it bubbled up towards her. *Will I be safe?* It did not matter the rain was coming down too fast now, she had to take shelter.

Crouched beneath the bridge, she rubbed her leg and noticed that she was bleeding. When she slipped on the bank, she must have cut herself on a branch or a stone. Her hands were muddy, but she tried to wipe away the blood. It did not look bad, but right then, she wished she were home, warm, dry, and safe by the fire. Why had she been so stupid?

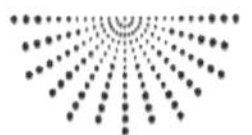

CHAPTER THREE

There is no one holy like the LORD;
there is no one besides you;
there is no Rock like our God.
— 1 Samuel 2:2

Jonas sat on his milking stool and lightly pulled on the cow's teats. Pull and squirt, pull and squirt, it was a gentle rhythm, and it always relaxed his nerves and made him feel better. When he was with his cows, he felt at ease as if the world was right, and nothing mattered. The only thing he loved more than his cows was cheese. Making cheese was a skill he learned from his *mamm*. Many years ago, she had let him follow her as she worked in the dairy, shaping and curing the cheese. It was a job that required infinite patience, and whenever he worked, he felt close to her.

Bella, the cow, mooed to let him know that he had stopped. Around this time every year, he found his mind drifting back. Remembering his *mamm* and how much he missed her. It would be ten years ago on Sunday when she collapsed and died in their dairy. The doctors had said it was an aneurysm and that nothing could be done. They said it was quick and painless and that he should take that as a blessing. But he never got to say goodbye, and he missed her every day. Then two years ago, his *daed* had decided that they needed a new start. They had moved from Ohio to Faith's Creek in Pennsylvania. It had been a difficult move, leaving behind all his friends, all his memories. At first, he thought it would be all right, but nothing was the same, even the Ordnung was different. Everyone here already had friends, and he seemed to become more and more isolated as each week drifted by.

Bella was finished, he picked up his pail and moved to the next cow. Gertrude was grumpy and kicked out as he sat next to her. He knew she would not hurt him, but she just liked to let him know who was in charge. Running a hand down her flank, he placed another pail beneath her and started to milk.

"Aren't you finished yet, boy?" Larry called.

"Not quite *Daed,* just got Gertrude to do."

Larry Schrock came and stood behind him, and Jonas could feel the glare of disappointment from his daed's eyes without even looking. He had been slow today. Spending too much time moping on the past and his *daed* would no doubt have more chores.

"I have something to discuss," Larry said as the wind whipped up outside and rattled the panels in the barn.

Gertrude moaned at the noise, but Jonas was nearly finished. With the last pull on each teat, she was dry. He picked up his bucket and stood. "Let me just let the girls out, and then we can talk."

"Of course, I will help," Larry said and walked to the other end of the barn.

One by one, they opened the stalls to let the cows loose and then taking a bucket of feed, Jonas walked in front of them and led them out to the pasture. It had started to rain, but the animals did not mind. They had trees and a barn for shelter if they needed it, but the water did not bother them, and they followed him to a trough. Once there, Jonas spread the food along the length so that all of his girls would get a mouthful. Then looking up at the dark and threatening sky, he headed back to the barn.

"What did you want, *Daed?*" he asked, trying to hide the trepidation that this had caused. If his *daed* wanted to talk, it would not be good. Nothing he seemed to do was good enough. Only last week, he had committed to the church, yet still, his *daed* moaned that he was not part of the community. That he kept himself to himself and spent more time with his cows and cheese than he did with their new neighbors.

"I think it is time you started courting," Larry said.

The words sent a cold spasm down Jonas' back and

made his breath catch in his throat. Jonas remembered how his *mamm* and *daed* were together. They were in love, deeply and completely, and he wanted that from a *fraa*. So far, none of the local girls had caught his eye, but if he was honest, he had only attended the after service singing on one occasion. It had been too uncomfortable to be amongst so many friends. To listen to them laugh and giggle while he stood on the outside. Suddenly Jonas realized that his *daed* was waiting for an answer. "I have not come across a girl who interests me, at least not yet."

"That is as I thought," Larry said. "That is why I have been talking to Mervin Esch. He has a *dochder* of courting age. Lucy, the girl's name is. A comely girl with *gut* manners and she can cook. You will pick her up tonight and go on a buggy ride with her. Then you will take her home after the service. Once you have been courting for a few months, we will get the Bishop to publish for you, and you can be married in November."

Jonas knew that his mouth was open, but he could not think of anything to say. As his brain tried to comprehend what had just happened, his mouth opened and closed like a door flapping in the wind.

At last, he got control of some of his faculties. "*Nee*," he said.

"You will not disobey me, boy, not while you live in this *haus*."

Jonas tried to remember what Lucy Esch looked like, and he could not. What was his *daed* doing? At that moment, he thought about leaving, about running away from the Amish way of life and starting again as an *Englischer*. Then he noticed that his *daed's* hands were shaking at his sides. Larry Schrock gave the impression that he was strong and capable, but his health had been failing recently. Jonas knew he was all the family he had here in Faith's Creek. If he left, now that he had committed to the church, then he would be shunned, and his father would be all alone. The stubborn old man, why did he have to push Jonas into a decision? Of course, if he was honest, he knew. His *daed* missed his *mamm* more than Jonas could understand and he wanted kin. A *fraa* for Jonas would bring grandchildren and family into their lives, and maybe Jonas could marry to give his *daed* that? But he couldn't, he wouldn't marry without love.

"Did you hear me, Jonas? You will court and marry this girl, or you will not live under my roof."

"*Nee Daed*, I won't." Jonas turned and walked out of the barn and into the rain. A walk would clear his head and allow him to calm down. Maybe he could even pray as he walked, and the Lord would clear the skies for him and show him the way.

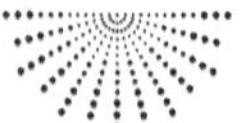

CHAPTER FOUR

But you, LORD, do not be far from me.
You are my strength; come quickly to help me.
Psalm 22:19

Lucinda Esch paced the house, waiting for her husband and eldest son to arrive home. Why had she let Lucy run off? If only she had followed her, then she would not be sitting here now, wondering what had become of the girl. At last, the horse and wagon pulled in and

Lucinda grabbed her coat and ran out to meet the men.

Mervin and Atlee climbed down from the wagon. They were soaked to the skin, but as they saw her face, all thoughts about the rain were gone.

"What is it?" Mervin asked as he raced towards his *fraa*.

"It is Lucy," Lucinda said. "I let it slip about Jonas, and she ran away. It was over an hour ago, and with this storm, I'm so worried. She was only wearing a light dress, what if something happened to her?"

Mervin pulled her into his arms and held her close. Quietly he soothed her hair as he tried to calm his own fear for his independent daughter. "She will be fine," he said and glanced at Atlee. "Now, which direction did she go?"

Atlee ran to the barn with the two Belgian draft horses. Quickly he turned them loose and saddled two fresh ones. They would be quicker on horseback and could go to more places. When he arrived back outside, his *daed* was ready.

"She headed into the wood," Mervin said. "I will follow; you go around by the road and come back towards us from the other side. Maybe we can find her between us."

Lucy crouched on the concrete, shivering. Why had she been so silly as to run away? If she had stayed and met this boy, then she could have found a reason for her *daed* not to like him, but instead, she ran off into the storm. Above the drain, the sky was almost black. The clouds covered the sun and threatened rain for many more hours. The wind howled through the trees, and the rain came down almost horizontally. Beneath her water rushed through a grate before disappearing beneath the bridge. At least she was sheltered, and maybe if she waited just a bit longer, she would be able to get home.

Closing her eyes, she tried to calm her racing heart and think of the best thing to do. She could not settle and stuck her head out to look at the sky. Instantly she was drenched, and she pulled herself back into the shelter. Her leg hurt, her clothes were covered in mud, and she was cold. There had to be a way out of here if only she could find it? If only she had a friend nearby? As soon as she had the thought, she found a smile on her face. Of course, she always had a friend, someone she could ask for help. Leaning back against the concrete, she closed her eyes and prayed for the rain to stop or for there to be some sign for her to follow. Instantly she started to feel better. The chill lifted from her skin, and her confidence rose until a pitiful cry interrupted her prayers. *What was that?*

Her eyes flew open, and she searched around in the gloom. The water still rushed past, the clouds kept the sky dark and gloomy. There was nothing there, but still, she heard it again. It was like an animal, small and scared as it cried for help. Maybe this was her sign; maybe this was why she was here?

Quickly she searched the area. There was nothing to see, so she closed her eyes again and stilled her mind. Listen, she told herself, let the sound come to you. There it was again. Weaker now and coming from the water. Lucy knelt down and moved towards the water's edge. It rushed through the drain, higher now and so fast that it seemed to have a mind of its own and even to be a living thing. Her eyes scoured the surface, and then she saw it. A small dark animal was clinging to the concrete on the opposite side of the drain.

Lucy felt her breath catch in her throat. She wanted to jump into the water. To rush across and rescue the creature, but something stopped her. Then she saw a branch coming towards the grate. If she went into the water, it would hit her, but if she didn't, maybe it would hit the poor creature and crush it against the metal.

Lucy gauged the distance and flattened herself back against the wall. The water was wide, but if she gave it everything she had, maybe she could clear it. There was no time to wait. She had asked for a sign, and this was what she got, it would be wrong to ignore it. Pushing forward with all she had, she leaped the water and seemed to hang in the air for minutes until, at last, she crashed down to the concrete. The log was getting closer, and she had no time to think. Her hand reached out and plucked the creature from the water just before the branch crashed into the grate.

Lucy looked down into golden, flecked eyes and realized that she was holding a bedraggled mottled brown kitten. The animal let out a mournful cry and tried to jump from her hands. Lucy was quick and she pulled it into her body, holding it firmly but not tight. As she held the little animal, it began to shiver, and she knew that she must get it home and warm. Peering out, she could see that it was still raining heavily. *What should she do?*

Holding the kitten gently, she used her apron to dry its coat as much as she could, then she held it against her, allowing her body heat to lift the chill from the creature. At last, it relaxed in her hands and purred gently. A smile came unbidden to her face. This was why she had run away. It had been *Gott's* will that she found this kitten, that she saved its life.

Jonas walked away from the farm. At times, he felt trapped by honor and duty. Many days he wondered what it would be like to go back into the *Englisch* world. It was something he had done for his *rumspringa*, and he had loved it. However, his *daed* had always brought him home with guilt. But marriage, he would not marry someone just because his *daed* thought it was time. Once again, the thought of leaving the community came to his mind. Why had he committed to the church? He loved *Gott* and did not need to commit to prove that, and now that he had committed, it made things even more difficult. If he hadn't committed, then he could leave the community and still visit his father, but now that he had committed, it meant that if he left, he would be shunned. As far as the community, the plain people were concerned if he left now, he was dead to them. And then his *daed* would be all alone. Why had they moved? They had friends back in Ohio and memories there, and once again, he regretted his *daed*'s decision to bring them to this place.

The rain pounded down on Jonas's back and dripped from his hat. He had walked half a mile before he realized just how soaked he was. The lane was running with water, and his clothes stuck to his skin, and just then, he started to laugh. His life was ruled by his father, and duty or honor would not let him leave. He closed his eyes and spun around in the lane. "Tell me what you want," he shouted up at the clouds. "Tell me what to do."

There was no answer, and he spun around, eyes closed, the rain falling on his face until he started to feel dizzy. Opening his eyes, he stared straight into the face of a horse, and a shout escaped him.

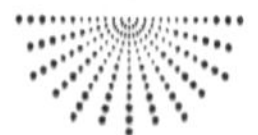

CHAPTER FIVE

But those who exalt themselves will be humbled,
and those who humble themselves will be exalted.
- Matthew 23:12

Jonas opened his eyes and was staring down a Dutch draft horse. The animal tossed its head and gave him a look of disdain. Jonas let out a yelp and leaped back, tripping over his feet and going down into the mud. The horse shook its head and stared down at him, and the next thing he knew, a strong hand hauled him to his feet.

"Are you Jonas?" the man asked.

"*Jah*," Jonas managed. "*Denke* for helping me."

"I need your help. My *dochder* Lucy has run away. She is out in this storm," Mervin said.

Jonas felt his brain come back to the situation. Lucy was the girl he was to court. He guessed she was not too happy about it either. "Of course," he said. What could he do to help? Where could she go? Then it came to him. "I know a place she could shelter. Come."

With that, he jumped into the wagon and turned the horse around. If he were out in this weather, he would go to the bridge. It was dry and out of the wind, and he had spent many an hour there throwing pebbles into the creek. One day he had seen a girl there. She was tall and slim and had a happy smile. For a second, he thought about going down and talking to her, but then he realized it would be inappropriate, and so he had gone home. As he drove the horse through the pouring rain, he hoped that it had been Lucy and that it was somewhere she would go.

"I want to *denke* for helping," Mervin called from his seat on the wagon.

Jonas concentrated on the road, but he knew that he must talk to this man. If things went to plan, they would be kin soon. "Of course, I will help," he said. "But maybe parents should not interfere in courting?" As soon as he said the words, he regretted them because he could see the guilt in the set of Mervin's shoulders and the deep bags under his eyes. "She will be fine," Jonas managed, cursing his loose tongue. "We are nearly there."

They arrived at the bridge. Jonas hauled on the reins pulling the horse to a halt. He jumped from the buggy before it fully stopped and raced down the bank. As soon as his feet touched the slippery slope, he slipped and started to slide down towards the water. A cry escaped him, and he tried to dig in his heels, but it was no use; he was going into the creek. Just before he slid into the water, a hand reached out and grabbed his shoulder and he turned and saw a bedraggled girl. Joy lit up his heart, he had found her but then he started to laugh. Her prayer *kapp* and dress were covered in mud. Her hair streamed down her face and her clothes were dirty and plastered to her body. "Lucy?" he asked, trying to stop the giggles.

"*Jah*," she said.

"I'm Jonas."

She was staring at him, and he noticed how intense her brown eyes were. Like liquid pools of coffee, they held his gaze. Of course, she was staring. He slipped down the slope, was rescued by a girl, and then he laughed at her. What was wrong with him? "Your *daed* is up there, we came to find you."

A **Few moments before:**

Lucy heard footsteps approaching and then a yelp of anguish. Next thing she knew, a man was slipping down the slope and heading for the water. Without even thinking, she reached out and grabbed onto his shoulder and hauled him around. As he turned, she looked into deep blue eyes that held her gaze and caused a flush to hit her cheeks. Where her hand held his shoulder, electricity crackled despite the wet and cold, and butterflies flapped their wings in her stomach. Her head dropped to hide her blushing, and then she heard him laugh. The first man she liked, and he was laughing at her.

"Lucy?" he asked through his giggles.

"*Jah*," she said, pulling her hand from his shoulder as if it had been stung.

"I'm Jonas," he said.

Lucy felt as if her world had been tugged out from beneath her. Not only had she seen something in those deep blue eyes, something she wanted to explore, but he had laughed at her, and now she finds out he was the man she must court.

"I'm sorry," Jonas said. "Here, let me help you out of here."

Gently he took her hand, and again, she felt a shock at the contact. Little fizzles of electric rose up her arm and into her heart. This was too much; she pulled her hand free and walked up the bank. "It is not me that fell," she called over her shoulder.

"Really," he said. "Then how did you get so dirty?"

How dare he? Lucy threw herself into her *daed's* arms, making sure that the kitten was not crushed between them. "I'm sorry," she said

"Never mind, let's get you home and dry and then a nice hot chocolate to warm you up."

The very sound of it was comforting, but as she pulled away, she could see Jonas, and he was laughing again. Maybe he thought she was too old for hot chocolate?

CHAPTER SIX

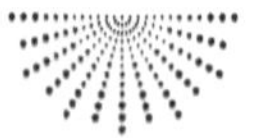

Now faith is confidence in what we hope for
and assurance about what we do not see.
- Hebrews 11:1

Lucy sat in the kitchen, her leg had been cleaned and bandaged, and she was wrapped in towels. A mug of hot chocolate steamed in front of her. Across the table, Jonas was also covered in towels, and he sipped at his own hot chocolate. Lucy was confused. Why did he keep laughing at her? Even now, there was a grin on his handsome face, and even though she wanted to stay angry, she found herself grinning in return.

"That is one of my favorite places," Jonas said.

"*Jah*, me too," she replied, enjoying how his eyes crinkled as he laughed again.

Lucy looked towards the sink where her *mamm* was cleaning the cat. Taking a quick sip of her chocolate, she smiled at Jonas and rocked in her chair. She desperately wanted to go over and check on her pet, but every time she did, her *mamm* scolded her, and she felt shame flush her cheeks. Jonas was horrible, all he did was laugh at her, but for some reason, she did not want him to think that she was just a silly little girl. "How is she?" Lucy asked.

Her *mamm* came over to the table. The look on her face froze Lucy's heart. More disappointment was coming. She handed the cat to her, and Lucy held it close. Now that the little animal was cleaned up, she could see how tiny it was. Wet bedraggled fur covered little more than bones, and its back leg was badly damaged. As she stroked the kitten, it's crying was replaced with a gentle purr. "*Mamm?*" Lucy asked her heart already broken.

"I'm sorry, Lucy, but the animal is too badly hurt. There is nothing we can do."

"But I could take her to David Byler, he is so *gut* with animals," Lucy said as tears ran down her face. Why would *Gott* do this to her? Let her save this creature and then take it away.

Her *daed* walked around the table, his face was gentle but firm. "The kitten is young and a stray. It is unlikely the treatment would work, and if it did, the animal would need constant care. I'm sorry, Lucy, but it is not possible."

"I will help," Jonas said. "I will take you, and I can help with the care."

Lucy felt a surge of love towards the disheveled man. Would he really do this for her? "Really?" she asked.

"*Jah*, come. If I can borrow your buggy, we will go now."

Mervin looked at his wife. It was plain to see that he wanted to say no, but something stopped him. Maybe this was *Gott's* will, he nodded. "Go, but be careful."

Soon they were dressed in clean, dry clothes and in

the buggy. The rain had stopped, and the roads were wet but not too treacherous.

"Is it too late to go?" Lucy asked.

"No, David will see you whatever the time. I have had to call on him for my cows before."

"Really?" Lucy said.

"*Jah*," Jonas said. "There is also a veterinary hospital if it is needed."

Lucy was shocked. Most Amish people were able to handle illnesses with their animals. There was always David who could cure most things, and it was rare that outside assistance was ever needed. The veterinary hospital was a long way away, too far in a buggy, and it was very expensive. She noticed that Jonas had a dreamy look in his eyes.

"We had a cow break her leg," he continued. "She was my favorite. I know it was silly because she was already old, but I had to save her. She came with us from Ohio."

"That is not silly," Lucy said. "I think maybe I could like you, after all."

Jonas pulled the horse to a halt and turned to look at her. His blue eyes shone in the dark, but his expression was earnest, and it caused her heart to flutter and her breath to grow short.

"I do not want to give you the wrong impression," Jonas said. "I will help with the cat because in some ways, it is my fault this happened. If you had not run away because of me, you would never have found the lucky animal."

"Lucky," Lucy said. "We should call her Lucky."

"*Jah*, it is a *gut* name," Jonas said. "Listen, Lucy, I do not wish to hurt you, but I will only marry for love. I will help you with this kitten, and I will pretend to court you to keep my *daed* happy, but I want you to know that I will not marry you. That would be wrong, and when one of us finds someone who could be our true love, then we are free to go our separate ways. Do you understand?"

Lucy nodded, it was what she had always dreamed of. All she wanted from a man was someone who loved animals as much as her and who made her heart leap. At first, she thought Jonas was horrible, but the fact that he had done this for her kitten made her realize that she could love him, and whenever she touched him, something happened. There were butterflies in her stomach and feelings that she could not explain. He was still staring at her, and his words had cut deep; she would show him. "Why would I want to marry a *mann* who laughs at me so much anyway?"

"I did not laugh, well not at you," he said, and as if to add insult to injury, he started laughing again. "It was just so funny," he said in between giggles.

Lucy turned back to the road. "Perhaps we should hurry."

CHAPTER SEVEN

As the body without the spirit is dead,
So faith without deeds is dead.
-James 2:26

Lucy handed the kitten over to David. She kissed its tiny black head, and her heart broke as its purring changed to cries of anguish as it was taken away. Would she ever see it again? Or would *Gott* take her pet from her once more? Jonas guided her back to the buggy, and they rode home in silence. Lucy could not believe how much she missed Lucky and how she wished she had waited there for her. Tomorrow was going to be a long day, and then she had to persuade her *daed* to lend her the buggy to go and pick the kitten up.

"I will pick you up tomorrow night," Jonas said as if he had read her thoughts.

"Really?" Lucy asked, and she began to feel a little better.

"Of course, if we are supposed to be courting, then it is something that I would do."

Lucy did not answer. Her delight at going to see her kitten was dampened by his uncaring attitude. For a second, she wanted to say don't bother, but then she wondered if her *daed* would let her go alone. She was stuck, and as she started to feel sad, she remembered the little kitten's golden eyes, and she felt warm. At last, she had a pet, and she sent a prayer to *Gott* to keep Lucky safe.

They were home and Lucy jumped down from the buggy. "*Denke*," she shouted as she ran into the house without looking back.

The next night Jonas picked her up. Lucy was quiet

as they made the long journey back to David's. She had prayed late into the night for her kitten, but the closer they got, the more worried she became. What if the kitten had died? It did not bear thinking about, and she tried to keep her faith, but still, the journey seemed so much longer.

"You are quiet," Jonas said.

"I did not realize you wanted to talk to me. After all, I am of no interest to you."

Jonas sighed. "I did not mean to insult you," he said. "Look, both of us were forced into this courtship, so why are you angry with me?"

"Because..." Lucy wanted to say *because I think I like you*, but she would not give him the satisfaction of seeing her hurt. So what could she say? The seconds ticked past. "Because you laughed at me when I was wet and dirty and looked a mess. I know I am not as pretty as many of the girls, but that is no reason to not want to get to know me." She wanted to stop talking, but now the words just kept coming. "You never mix with us, maybe you think you are too *gut* for us, and maybe that is why you laughed at me when I was down. Well, because of that, I do not wish to get to know you either. I think we should tell our folks that this is not working, don't you?"

Jonas turned towards her, and his face was no longer mocking, in fact, if anything, it looked hurt.

"I do not want to do that. It would hurt my *daed*," he said. "Did you know that my *mamm* died ten years ago?"

Lucy did not, and she felt a flush of guilt. Maybe that was why he was so grumpy with her, he was missing his *mamm*.

"As the anniversary comes up," Jonas said "my *daed* always gets so sad. He tries not to show it, but it is around this time he always wants me to court. Can we please keep up this ruse for a couple of months?"

"I am sorry," Lucy said. "I did not know about your mamm. Maybe we could get to know each other and see how things go. You may find I am not so bad." Lucy waited for him to answer, and as the seconds ticked by, she felt her confidence slipping.

"We're here," Jonas said.

Thoughts of courting were gone from Lucy's mind, she jumped from the buggy and ran into the house.

avid handed her a box. "This is one strong little kitten," he said. He gave them some milk substitute and bandages and explained what needed doing. The kitten would need constant care, just as her *daed* had said. At last, he looked down at Lucy with serious brown eyes that filled her heart with fear.

"If she does not get better in the next day, then there is nothing more I can do," David said as gently as he could.

Lucy felt as if she had been kicked by a horse. The air rushed from her lungs, and her stomach clenched. "Then what can be done?"

David rubbed a hand through his hair, and his eyes searched the ceiling. "It would be a kindness to let her go, but you can pray that she heals."

Jonas guided Lucy back to the buggy, and they rode home in silence. "I will pray for you," he said as he dropped her off. "There is still hope."

CHAPTER EIGHT

*The LORD, your God, is with you, he is mighty
to save.
He will take great delight in you,
he will quiet you with his love,
he will rejoice over you with singing.
- Zephaniah 3:17*

Lucy spent the night caring for Lucky. Every two hours, she prepared the kitten some of the special milk, and she made sure that she was warm and comfortable. As the kitten slept in her arms, she prayed that *Gott* would keep her safe and that maybe Jonas would start to see her as more than just a burden.

The following day she took Lucky with her as she completed her chores, only leaving her alone for very short periods of time. The kitten was looking no better, yet she lifted her head and purred every time Lucy came near.

"You are spoiling that cat," her *mamm* said as they passed in the kitchen, but Lucy could see by her smile that she did not mean it.

After they had eaten, Lucy took Lucky into the back room and sat with her. She was almost in tears as she knew that the kitten would not survive when there was a knock on the door. Lucy looked up; it was Jonas.

"May I come in?" he asked.

Lucy could see her *mamm* behind him. "Leave the door open," her *mamm* said and smiled at her daughter.

Lucy waited until her *mamm* had gone. "What do you want?" she asked.

"We are courting," Jonas said. "I wanted to spend time with you."

"Well, you can pick me up for service on Sunday and drive me home after night singing. There really is no need to see me every day." Even though she was angry with him, she felt good that he had come. Her emotions seemed to chase their tail like a silly dog as they went around and around in her mind.

"I'm sorry," Jonas said. He was holding his hat and looking down at his feet. "How is Lucky?"

Lucy looked down at the tiny bundle of fur. The kitten was weaker now, and Lucy knew that she would not survive. "I think I am losing her," she said, holding on to the kitten.

"I hope not," Jonas said. "Let us pray for her together, and maybe she will be fine."

Jonas knelt down, and Lucy knelt beside him. She felt good that he had come, and as they started to pray, her mind relaxed for the first time since she had found the kitten. "Show me a way, Lord?" she asked but nothing came to mind. It did not matter; she prayed and let go. *Gott* would find a way, he would make things right. "Amen," she said, and Jonas joined in.

She looked at him, and it felt good to have him here. At least she was not alone with her grief, but she noticed that Jonas was fidgeting.

"I have to go," he said. "I just thought of something... Lucy, do not look so disappointed I will be back soon."

With that, he ran from the room, and Lucy let her tears fall. Gently she picked Lucky up and cradled the tiny kitten in her lap. As the emptiness of the room seemed like a weight on her shoulders, she made a decision. In a couple of hours, she would ask her *daed* to take her to see David, and they would let Lucky go.

As they started to pray, Jonas was overwhelmed by Lucy's strength and determination. She cared so deeply for this animal that she would do anything to keep it safe. A laugh almost escaped him; wasn't that what he wanted from a *fraa?* Someone who cared for animals as much as he did? The more he saw of Lucy, the more he admired her, and right now, he would do anything to take away her pain. "Show me the way, Lord?" he whispered, and almost immediately, he thought of the veterinary center over in Bird in Hand. It was over an hour away by buggy ride and that would be too much for the kitten to face, so how could he get there? The answer came to him and he wanted to jump up and run out. It would be best to not tell Lucy until he was sure that he could organize this. Still, a smile crossed his face and he needed to go now.

"I have to go," he said. "I just thought of something... Lucy, do not look so disappointed I will be back soon."

Jonas ran from the room and jumped into his buggy. It was just a quick ride to Bishop Amos Beiler's house, and he hoped that he could ask this favor. Setting the horse to a gallop, he swung into the yard and hauled to a halt.

"Where's the fire boy?" the Bishop called as he came out of his barn.

"Sorry, Amos," Jonas said. "I wondered if I could use the phone."

Amos Beiler's eyebrows drew down tight, and Jonas was sure he would say no.

"And why would you need to do that?" Amos asked.

Jonas explained as quickly as he could. Amos nodded and steered him into the phone shanty near the barn.

"If this *Englischer* does not help you," Amos said. "I have a friend who will."

Jonas thanked him, and for the first time in two years, he realized that he was home. This was his community if he would just accept it. They had not been pushing him out; it was him that had stayed on the sidelines. "*Denke*," he said, and then he dialed the number of John Sharpe an *Englischer* he had worked for last summer. A man that was very grateful when he saved his daughter from drowning.

"John, it is Jonas," he said, and then he explained what he needed.

"Be at your girl's house in thirty minutes," John said.

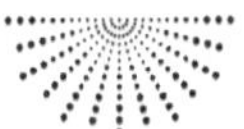

CHAPTER NINE

But you, dear friends, by building yourselves up in
your most holy faith and praying in the Holy Spirit,
– Jude 1:20

Jonas drove his horse back to Lucy's and ran in all excited. "Get Lucky ready," he said.

Lucy walked out of the backroom; her eyes were red and full of tears. "Ready?" she asked as her lip quivered, believing that this was the end.

"*Jah*," Jonas said. "A car is coming; we can take her to the veterinary hospital in town."

"That is too expensive for a stray cat," Lucy's *daed* said.

Lucy looked down at her hands. "I have made over a dozen quilts," she said at last. "I could sell them at the market, and maybe I would have enough to pay for the operation."

"*Jah*, I'm sure you would," Jonas said, "but I will pay."

"Why would you do that?" Lucy asked.

Jonas looked at her, and his blue eyes seemed as deep and intriguing as a clear blue sky. It was as if she were pulled into their depths and comforted by what she saw there.

"I worked for a rich *Englisch mann* for over a year," Jonas said. "He paid me very well, and he taught me something that I will never forget. He said to me that helping a friend is the best investment that you can ever make. It will always pay you back in ways more fabulous than money. I have seen the way you care for that kitten, and I believe that you are the sort of person I would like to be my friend. Let me do this for you."

Lucy found that she was breathless again, and she could not say anything, so instead, she just nodded and picked up her Bible. At last, the words came. "Will you pray with me, Jonas?"

"I would love to," he said.

Together they bowed their heads and prayed for the little kitten until the sound of a car arriving dragged them to their feet.

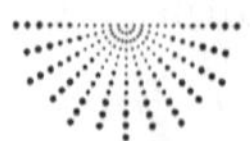

CHAPTER TEN

"You expected much, but see, it turned out to be little.
What you brought home, I blew away. Why?"
declares the LORD Almighty.
"Because of my house, which remains a ruin,
while each of you is busy with his own house."
– Haggai 1:9

They traveled to the hospital in silence. It was Lucy's first time in a car, and she was excited, nervous, and terrified that even after this, Lucky may still die. As they walked in, it was so bright and new. It looked to her like a people's hospital with the white and green walls and seats where people sat waiting. A woman with her blonde hair on top of her head and make-up greeted them and took their details. Then she handed Lucky over and was told to come back in four hours. Everything was a daze, and as Jonas steered her outside, she wondered if she would ever see the kitten again.

The car drove them home in silence, and the driver agreed to collect them later.

"I can wait with you if you like," Jonas said. "We can pray together."

"I would like that, but don't you have work to do?"

"It is all right," Jonas said. "A few friends and neighbors agreed to help out so that I could be with my girl."

Lucy felt a blush hit her cheeks at the words, but then she realized that it was just for show. The disappointment was like a bucket of cold water poured over her head. She imagined what it would be like if they were really courting. Having Jonas here made things easier. In fact, she knew that she could cope with anything as long as he was by her side. Then she started to cry. He wasn't with her. The only reason he was here was to please his *daed*.

Jonas put an arm around her shoulder and pulled her to him. "Do not cry, my love," he whispered. "Have faith in *Gott*, and Lucky will be fine. She is in the best hands, and soon you will see her."

The words were comforting, and slowly, Lucy stopped crying and wiped away her tears. She pulled herself free and moved over to the fireplace. "Will you pray with me?" she asked.

"Of course," Jonas said. They knelt on the floor and prayed for the little kitten that had been so lucky that Lucy found it just at the right moment.

The praying calmed Lucy, and she began to feel better. "Will you talk to me?" she asked.

Jonas talked, he told her about his cows and how much he loved cheese. Then he told her how he once dreamed of leaving the community. Of the *Englisch* man that he worked for and how he was unsure about his life and what it held for him.

As he talked about his life outside the community, Lucy saw wistfulness in his eyes. It made her sad.

Maybe this was why he did not find her interesting? Maybe he wanted to leave the community and was just giving his *daed* a little more time.

"It is time," *Mamm* said as she stuck her head into the room.

All through the journey back, Lucy tried to think of something to say, but she could not compete with all the strange things he had told her about. The more she thought about it, the more she realized she didn't want to. All she wanted was for Lucky to be all right and to find a man that could love her. One who would cause her to feel like she did when she looked into Jonas's eyes.

"You seem quiet," Jonas said. "Do not worry, Lucky will be fine, and I will help you nurse her back to health."

"That would make me very happy," she said, and she felt her heart melt as he winked at her and took her hand.

The car pulled into the car park.

The receptionist smiled at her when she ran in, and Lucy knew it was good news. She sat on the hard chair with Jonas next to her and the wait was torture. Her heart leaped against her chest, and she was finding it hard to breathe. Then a man walked in. In his arms was a bundle, held against his white coat. With a smile, he walked over and handed Lucy the bundle. Lucky was wrapped up inside. Her eyes only just open.

"You will need to feed her every two hours and make sure that the wound is dressed and kept clean," he said. "If you have any problems, come back straight away. Otherwise, she should be fine."

Then he handed her the bill. Lucy's hand shook as she tried to turn it over, but Jonas took it from her, and with a smile, he walked over to the receptionist. Lucy watched as he handed over a lot of notes andshe wondered how she would ever pay him back.

"We can go now," Jonas said.

"*Denke*, I will pay you back," Lucy said as she carried Lucky back to the car.

Jonas helped her in, as his hand touched her arm, she

felt the electricity spark between them. It was a good feeling and left her smiling as he climbed in next to her.

"That is not necessary," Jonas said. "We are courting, after all." He winked at her, and the driver smiled at them both and set the car on the path to home.

Lucy could not stop the pounding of her heart that his wink had caused. How could something so simple set her pulse racing and leave her feeling as if she had just sprinted up the hill behind their barn? That was when she realized that she was falling for this quiet man. It was such a shame that he felt nothing for her.

Lucy held on to the kitten, her heart was filled with joy, and also breaking. Jonas wanted to leave the community. All these years, she had been looking for love. At last, she finds it, only to find that the man wanted to leave. What should she do?

"You are very quiet," Jonas said. "I thought you would be happy."

"I am happy," she said. "Lucky is lucky because of your help, she will live."

"Because of both of us," he said.

Lucy sat back in the car; she did not want to talk. It seemed as if *Gott* was giving with one hand and taking with the other, and she could not cope with the emotions. Soon they were home. "*Denke,*" she said as she jumped out of the car. "I will see you Sunday morning."

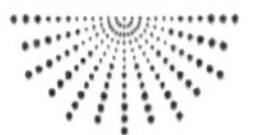

CHAPTER ELEVEN

Peacemakers who sow in peace raise a harvest of
righteousness.
- James 3:18

Jonas thanked the driver and stood outside Lucy's house. It was obvious that she didn't want to see him, it made him feel bad. Slowly he turned and started the walk home. What was wrong with him? One day he wanted their courtship to be just pretend. But now, when Lucy behaved as if it meant nothing to her, he is…? What was he? It was neither anger nor disappointment, but he was feeling something and it made his head spin.

The sound of a horse made him step off the road.

"*Gut* day Jonas," Bishop Beiler called down from his buggy. "Would you like a ride?"

"*Jah*," Jonas said and hopped up onto the buggy.

"How is your girl's kitten?" Amos asked.

"It is *gut*," Jonas said. "Bishop, I have a problem."

"Call me, Amos. Now, talk to me and let us see if we can solve it."

Jonas took off his hat and ran a hand through his hair. It was so hard to know where to start. "My *daed* made me court Lucy Esch. I did not want to because I wanted to marry for love."

"I understand," Amos said.

"I told Lucy this, and she was angry. But I have been a *gut* boyfriend. I have helped her with the kitten, and now she doesn't want to talk to me. I don't understand what I have done wrong."

"Have you prayed on this?" Amos asked.

"I do not know what to pray for. What to ask for," Jonas said.

"Are you sure," Amos answered, and there was wisdom in the glint of his eyes. "Are you sure that you have not found what you were looking for?"

Jonas felt a rush of freedom and the excitement that he had only ever felt before when he thought about leaving. "Maybe," he said, "but have I spoilt things? Can I make things right?"

"That is easy," Amos said. "Speak your heart and pray on it." The Bishop pulled the horse to a halt. "Do you wish to be taken anywhere?"

"*Nee, denke*, I can run."

With that, Jonas turned around and ran back towards Lucy's house. How could he have been so stupid? He just hoped that he was not too late.

As he knocked on the door, he prayed that she would speak to him, and he realized how cruel he had been. In fact, he had been arrogant and uncaring.

"Jonas," Lucy said as she answered the door. "What did you want?"

Seeing her sweet face made his tongue fill his mouth like an old boot and froze the words in his throat. Standing there, with a grin on his face, he got nervous and started to giggle. Lucy's smile slipped, and her face showed hurt. Of course, once again, she must think that he was laughing at her. Still, the giggles would not stop, but Lucy started to close the door.

"I'm sorry," he managed. "I giggle when I'm nervous."

Lucy stepped out of the door and closed it behind her. "Jonas, I will be forever in your debt for what you did for Lucky, but what do you want now?"

Jonas took a deep breath and whispered a prayer, "Please *Gott* let me speak." Then he cleared his throat. "I wanted to tell you how much I admire you," he said, "and also how much I enjoy our time together. I have been looking for a girl that loves animals as I do and that I find easy to talk to. I love spending time with you and look forward to helping you... What I'm trying to say is that I would like to court you… It is no longer because of my *daed*. It is because I love you." The words just came out of him, but as soon as they did, he knew it was true. He loved her for her courage and strength, and he wanted to spend his life with her.

Tears were running down Lucy's face.

"I'm sorry," he said. "I did not mean to make you cry."

"I love you too," she said. "How could I not love the *mann* who saved my kitten?"

"Then you will court me, for real?" he asked.

"*Jah*," she said. "But the next few weeks will have to be spent looking after a certain kitten."

Jonas laughed again and hugged her tight. Letting her go, he looked into her eyes and said, "That kitten is not the only one that is lucky."

Just as their parents had planned, the couple courted for a few months. They found they had much in common apart from their love of animals. Jonas began to mix more as Lucy introduced him to her friends and relatives, and in November, their marriage was published.

Lucy had everything she wanted. A true love with a man who made her pulse race every time she saw him and a beautiful mottled brown cat called Lucky.

Jonas no longer thought about leaving. He had all the love and excitement he could ever need, and he had friends.

At last, he felt at peace in his new home, and he thanked *Gott* for his one true love.

I hope you enjoyed this book as much as I enjoyed writing it. True love is something that we should all experience. I am lucky that I found my true love, Martin. We are just as much in love today as when we first met. I thank God for bringing us together and wish each and every one of you finds their own true love, their soul mate.

Sending you all my Love,

Sarah.

It was the first time in the past year that any of them could breathe, really breathe. Zook... Rebecca hated it, almost as much as she hated Rebecca. Yet that didn't matter. It would be their new last name as Rebecca was her new first name.

Anger and fear fought for control as she thought of all she would miss. She had just turned 16, and now she had to leave it all behind, everything. Her friends, school, boys, parties, everything including her own name was gone. For a moment, she thought of her mom, kind eyes and a sweet smile filled her mind. They were so much alike, both tall and slim with honey blonde hair and blue eyes, but she would never see her again. How could that be? How could someone so filled with love be gone so quickly, so instantly and so horribly? The thoughts threatened to choke her, but she shook them away. It was too painful, even now. But that was not the worst of it.

"Maybe it will be fun," Eli said.

"Fun? You only think it's fun because you're a kid and you don't have any friends yet," Rebecca said mentally calling him Eli in her mind like the Marshal told them.

"Hey, I'm not a kid. I'm in double digits now, just like you. I can make my own decisions, and I can think for myself. I do think this will be fun. I think it'll be awesome, not just fun but awesome."

Even looking at her brother seemed to make her mad. Cody, no don't call him that even to yourself. The words of the Marshal rang in her ears and seemed to make her blood boil. It was so unfair. Eli, as her brother was now called, looked more like their dad, he would be strong and broad, and he had thick black hair that stood up at all different angles. Right now, he looked stupid in his black pants, suspenders, and white shirt. Even the straw hat made her want to laugh. A cringe went through her as she remembered what she was wearing. *Could this get any worse?*

"Keep living in your little fantasy world, Eli. There's nothing awesome about this," Rebecca almost spat the words out. "I bet after a week of not playing your stupid little video games you're going to be balling your eyes out and begging to go back home. Begging to go back to our crappy little apartment in our crappy old city."

"Don't be so hard on your little brother, Rebecca. He's only ten. And besides, I think it could be fun."

"Really Dad? After everything that's happened, after everything you've done, after Mom, and now this, how you can say this could possibly be fun?"

Aaron took a deep breath, but he did it like an expert, one used to trying to hide the frustration and anger he was feeling. If only he could've done that when it really mattered, but what Rebecca said stung. It stung like the biggest, meanest yellow jacket he had ever seen when he was just a kid playing on a playground in his hometown. He remembered the venom that yellow jacket sunk into his arm. It was the worst feeling he could remember, but this was more punishing because it was all true.

"Well, I do think this it's a little cool, that we get to ride in a horse-drawn buggy with real horses," Rebecca's younger sister Lydia added.

"Oh, please. Haven't you noticed that smell? That's not air freshener you know. That's horse crap, just like our life, crap, and it keeps falling down on us every so often. I promise you, you're both going to hate this in a few weeks, probably sooner."

Lydia just sighed and put her head back into her journal. At thirteen, she didn't talk much and kept her nose in a book scribbling or writing at all times. It annoyed Rebecca because she thought they should stick together. After all, Lydia had lost her mother too. A lock of brown hair had escaped Lydia bonnet and furled on her cheek. Lydia was a strange mix of both parents. She had Dad's brown eyes and auburn hair that had blonde streaks in the sunshine. Once she had always been happy, but since their mom's death, she had been so withdrawn.

"Rebecca, just give it a chance," Dad's voice wavered, he hadn't even convinced himself. "This is our new life now. We have a real opportunity here if we just let ourselves see where it takes us. We need to learn to make the most of it."

"And why is that Dad? Why is that? Tell me? Why do we need this new godforsaken opportunity? You messed up, you always do. You're such a loser, Dad. You say you're so smart, but there's nothing smart about you. I don't see what Mom ever saw in you, and now she's dead. You killed her. You killed her!" Rebecca felt her voice rise as the pain took over. A vision of flying blood, of Mom falling and the explosive sound of a gunshot, filled her mind. Again she shook it away. Before it brought tears to her eyes. That sign of weakness, it would be too much to bear. No one could see her cry, not now, not ever.

"Hey, that's not fair. I didn't kill your Mom. I had no control over that bullet that came into our home," Aaron's voice trailed off as if he didn't believe it himself.

Sensing his weakness Rebecca pounced. "Don't give me that. You know good and well it's your fault. If you hadn't been doing what you were doing... Mom worked so hard, so hard to take care of us, to feed us, and what were you doing? Playing poker, playing the horses, playing all your stupid little games, just like Cody... oh sorry, Eli." Sarcasm burst out from her rant, he had it coming. Rebecca continued before he had a chance to defend himself. "ELI..." she yelled, "Eli didn't use our money. He didn't borrow someone else's money. He didn't go out and get drunk and do all those stupid things... but you did."

"Listen, I know I've made a lot of mistakes, but I...."

"Mistakes? Mistakes!" Rebecca repeated.

"I worked too. I had a job too. I wasn't just sitting at home watching television all the time," Aaron's voice almost pleaded.

Eli's head was down and he looked close to tears. Rebecca hated herself, but she couldn't seem to stop. The words had a life of their own and had to be said. They ripped out of her like a hurricane. For a second she wondered what damage they would cause, but still she couldn't stop them.

"Well, that would've been better. At least, if you didn't have a job and you were just a lazy bum, you wouldn't have gambled away the rest of Mom's money, but you did. Didn't you? You spent all the money from your sorry little part-time job."

"I did the best I could."

"The best you could? Really? You got fired from your last job because you came in drunk. You only had that job because of Mom's old boyfriend from high school. You've been a drunk as long as I can remember. Here's a thought. Why didn't you ever think to stop drinking and actually do something productive with your life?"

"Stop it. You're hurting my ears," Eli shouted as he put his hands over his ears.

"You are a little loud, Rebecca," Lydia added as she continued doodling on her tiny sketchbook to while away the long ride.

"A little loud? A little loud? How about this? Is this loud enough for you? You're a loser, Dad, a loser. I swear you killed her. You killed mom. Mom. It's your fault, but you should be the one who's dead, not her. You Dad, I wish you were dead. I wish you were the one that got shot and not her, then we would be happy, then everything would be okay."

Her screams rose over the clanking of the hooves and gravel that carried them closer to their destination and drew a few curious stares.

"I know honey," Aaron said. "Everything you said was right and I'm sorry, and all I can say is that I promise I will do better... I'm sorry."

Rebecca's screams were short-lived, after those words and the defeat she saw on her father's face, her yells quieted to a stream of tears. The water poured from her eyes, mixing with what ran from her nose. Feeling so tired, it hurt to move; she wiped it away with the back of her hands.

"Ew, gross," Eli said.

"Shut up. Leave me alone. Go back to doing whatever it is that you're doing in that little head of yours."

"Dad, she just told me to shut up, and she's been yelling all this time. Tell her to be quiet," Eli said to his dad.

"Rebecca, you do need to keep it down. If someone overhears you, you know what that means for us." Aaron couldn't say much else, at least not about what Rebecca said. What could he possibly say? That she was right, that he was a loser, a disappointment, a gambler, a drunk, a poor father? That he had killed the woman he loved? She was right, every word, and every sentence. He had blown every opportunity he ever had in his entire life. That's what he did.

He had such promise as a child, the top of his class in school. He wasn't just smart. He was brilliant. His teachers knew he was going to get accepted into the best schools and have it paid for, but like everything else in his life, he screwed it up. He took every shiny new opportunity, and found a way to mess up even the easiest sure thing, and his full scholarship at the University of Pennsylvania -- lost. His first job after finishing -- lost his second job after finishing high school -- lost. All of them went to pieces. That's when he started drinking and after all his failures, they had ended up here.

Running for their lives and hiding out in a tiny hamlet called Faith's Creek. What did he know about the Amish? How could he ask his children to live like this? Again and again, he had tried to think of another way but he could not find one. If they wanted to stay alive, they had to live here. With no electricity, no computers, and no cars for at least a year. His children had lost their mother and now they had lost their friends and their lifestyle, all because of him.

There was nothing he could say to his daughter, his beautiful Christy... *No, call her Rebecca.* There was nothing he could say to Rebecca... because she was right.

Get this amazing value box set for FREE with Kindle Unlimited Amish Faith and Love 15 Book Box Set.

This book is dedicated to the wonderful Amish people and the faithful life that they live.

Go in peace, my friend.

Sarah Miller was born in Pennsylvania and spent her childhood close to the Amish people. Weekends were spent doing chores, quilting, or eventually babysitting in the community. She grew up to love their culture and the simple lifestyle and had many Amish friends. The one thing that you can guarantee when you are near the Amish, Sarah believes, is that you will feel close to God.

Many years later she married Martin, who is the love of her life and moved to England. There she started to write stories about the Amish. Recently after a lot of persuasion from her best friend, she has decided to publish her stories. They draw on inspiration from her relationship with the Amish and with God, and she hopes you enjoy reading them as much as she did writing them. Many of the stories are based on true events, but names have been changed, and even though they are authentic at times, artistic license has been used.

Sarah likes her stories simple and to hold a message, and they help bring her closer to her faith. She currently lives in Yorkshire, England, with her husband Martin and seven very spoiled chickens.

She would love to meet you on Facebook at https://www.facebook.com/SarahMillerBooks

Sarah hopes her stories will both entertain and inspire, and she wishes that you go with God.